The Chocolate Train Story

A MAGICAL TALE

DAVID STEVEN WILLIAMS

To order additional copies of this book, contact:
Xlibris
UK TFN: 0800 0148620 (Toll Free inside the UK)
UK Local: 02 0369 56328 (+44 20 3695 6328 from outside the UK)
www.xlibrispublishing.co.uk
Orders@ Xlibrispublishing.co.uk

ISBN: Softcover   978-1-6641-1759-4
        EBook   978-1-6641-1760-0

Print information available on the last page

Rev. date: 04/05/2022

Dedication Page

This book is dedicated to the love of my life - my two sons Aston and Joseph.

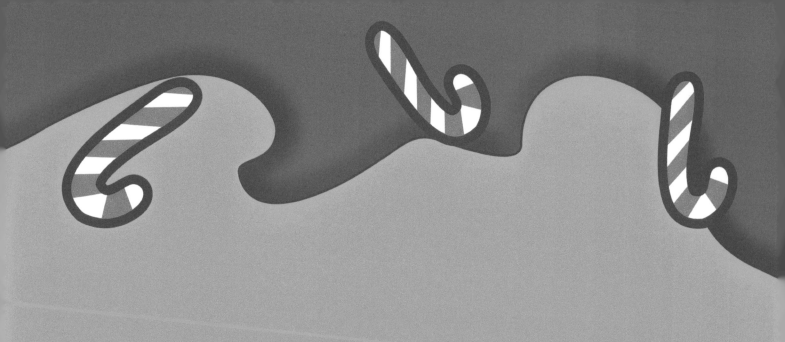

Once upon a time, there were two little boys called Aston and Joseph. Aston and Joseph were going on a school trip to the park - they were both very excited and rushed to get ready! When they arrived at school, the boys and all of their friends got on the big school bus to go to the train station.

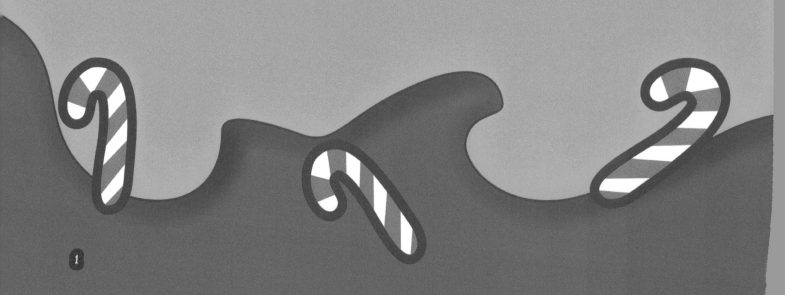

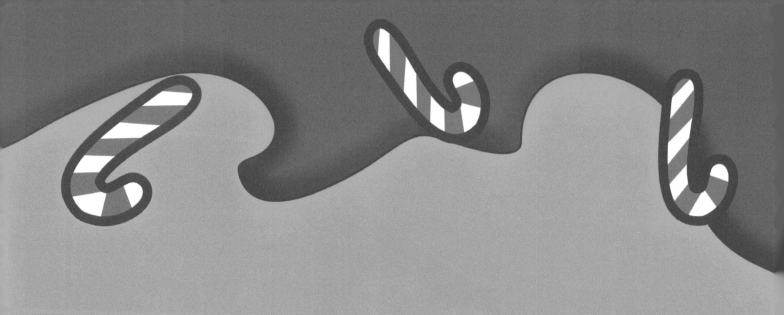

Everyone waited patiently for the train to come. Choo choo! Choo choo! Choo choo! Choo choo! Choo choo! 'Do you hear that?' Aston asked Joseph. 'Yes, it's our train!' replied Joseph. As the train pulled up to the platform Joseph said 'WOW! It's a steam train!'. But this was no ordinary steam train... this was a magical steam train!

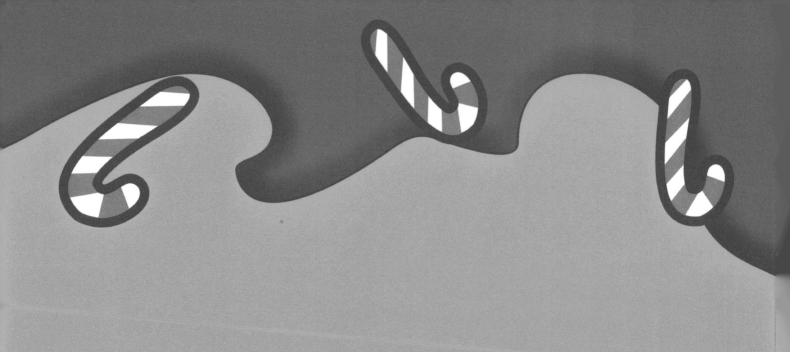

All of the children got on and it started to pull away from the station. Choo choo! Choo choo! Choo choo! Choo choo! Choo choo! The train started to go faster and faster and faster!

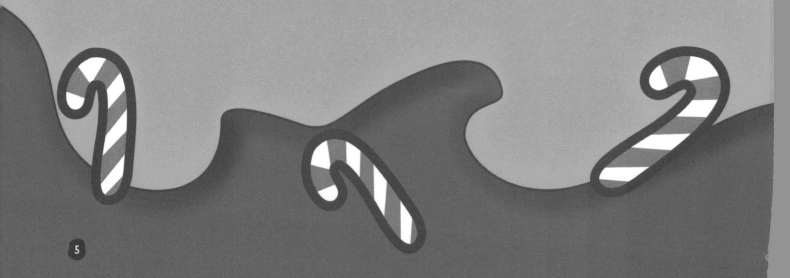

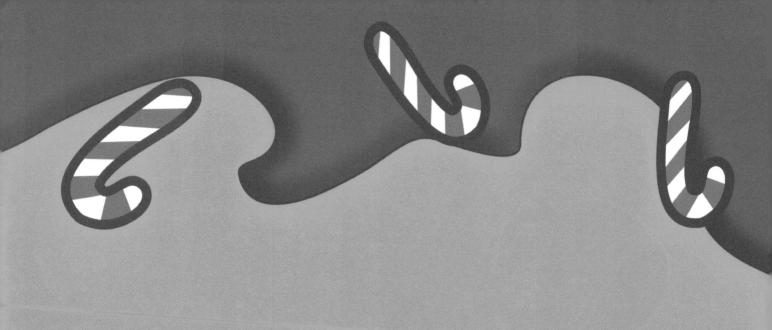

Just as it reached its top speed, it entered a tunnel. Suddenly, everything went pitch black and there was a very loud bang.

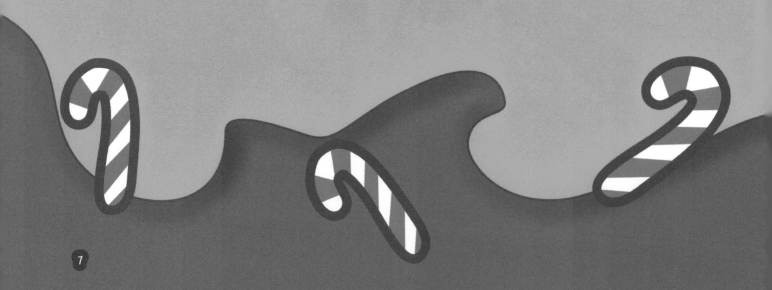

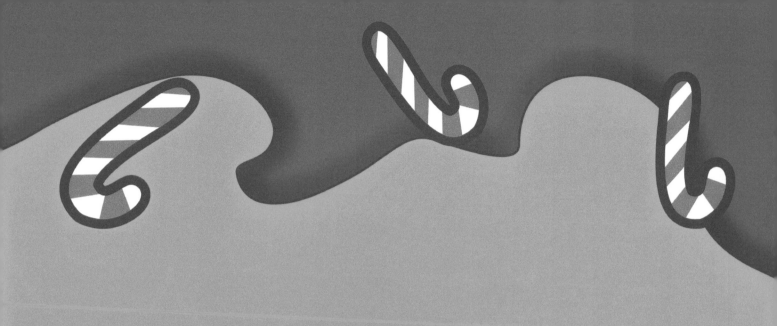

Everyone wondered what had happened. When they came out of the other side of the tunnel, the children couldn't believe their eyes - everything had turned into chocolate, cake and ice cream! The cars, the houses and even the train had turned into sweeties and chocolate.

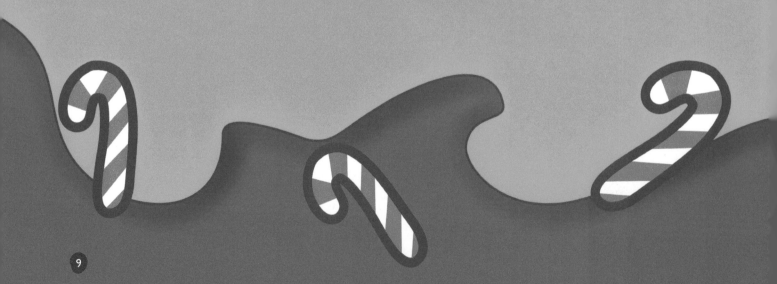

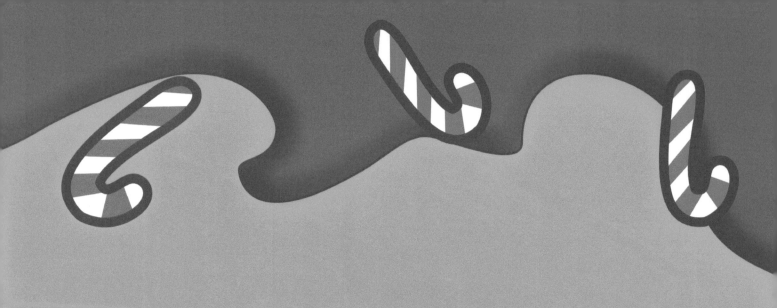

Eventually, the chocolate train pulled into the chocolate station and all of the children got off and walked to the park. They were supposed to spend the whole day having fun at the park, but when the children got there, instead of playing, they started to eat everything! They ate the sweetie swings, the runny chocolate roundabout, the chocolate sauce slide, the ice cream climbing frame... They ate everything! They were so greedy there was nothing left for them to play on!

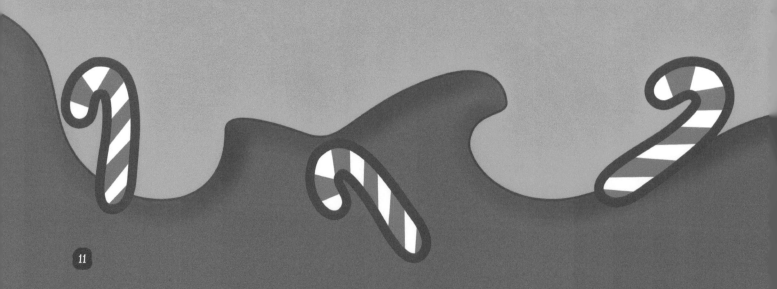

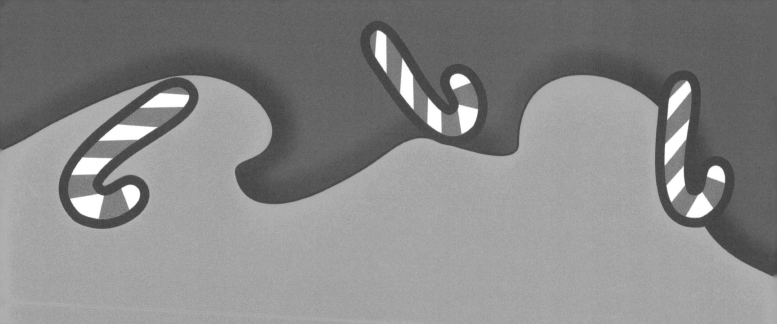

All the children were so full that their tummies began to hurt, but because they were so greedy, they didn't stop until everything was gone! Everyone walked back to the train station and got on the magical chocolate train.

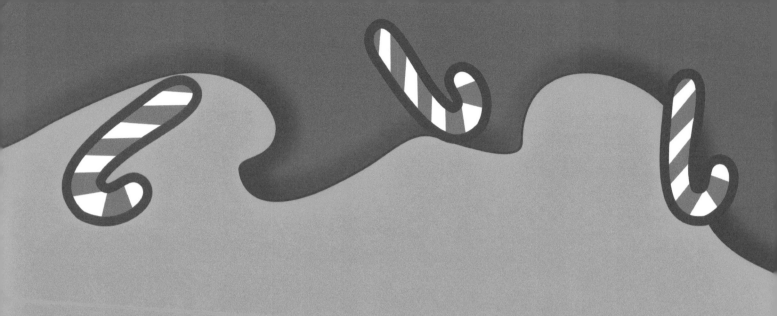

It pulled away from the station and started going faster and faster and faster! Choo choo! Choo choo! Choo choo! Choo choo! Choo choo! The train entered the tunnel and there was another bang, and everything went pitch black! Everyone gasped, and wondered 'what was that?'

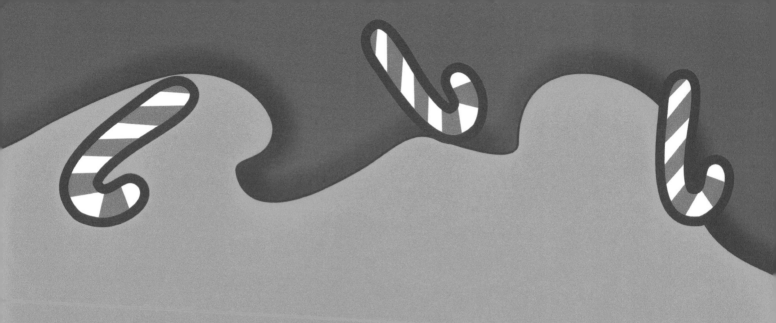

Before long, they came out of the tunnel and everything had changed back to normal. All the houses and cars... everything was the same as it usually was.

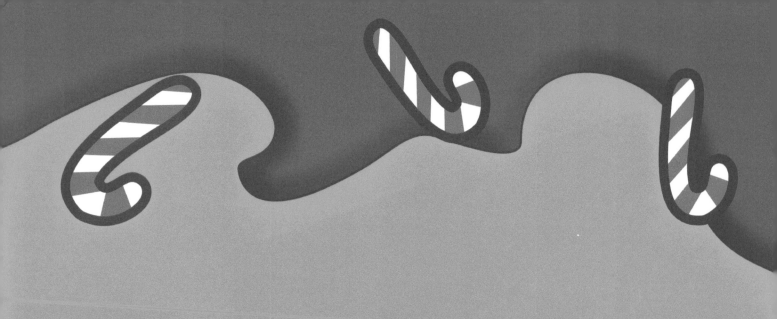

The children got back on the big school bus and returned to school. At the end of the day, Aston and Joseph's mummy and daddy came to pick them up. Aston and Joseph told them all about their big adventure on the chocolate train and their trip to the chocolate park.

But they didn't believe them! Aston and Joseph had chocolate all around their mouths, so they knew it was real!